Hot Wheels™

Off-Roading

By Ace Landers

Illustrated by Ed Wisinski and Dave White

SCHOLASTIC INC.
New York Toronto London Auckland Sydney
Mexico City New Delhi Hong Kong Buenos Aires

ISBN-13: 978-0-545-02018-3
ISBN-10: 0-545-02018-2

Published by Scholastic Inc. SCHOLASTIC and associated logos are trademarks and/or registered trademarks of Scholastic Inc.

25 24 23 22 21 20 14 15/0

Printed in the U.S.A. 40
First printing, February 2008

It is race day. It is raining.

The racers will drive on a dirt road.

The racers are ready to go.

The wheels spin quickly.

The racers speed up the trail.

The windshield gets splashed with dirt.

These racers are tough!

Some racers get stuck in the mud.

The other racers head up the mountain.

The mountain is big. There are many turns on the course.

Some racers get flat tires.

At the top of the mountain,
the racers drive through snow.

The green truck moves
close to the trees.

The blue truck slides in the snow.

The green truck passes the blue truck!

Each racer wants to be in the lead.

The first one to finish will win the race.

Some racers take short cuts.

The green truck drives
around the trees.

This truck blasts past the others.

The blue truck misses a turn.
It spins out of control!

The other racers drive down the mountain.

The weather is better on this side.

Some trucks take risky turns!

The yellow racer is going too fast!

Oh, no! The yellow racer lands in quicksand!

A rescue team helps the driver.

The finish line is over the hill.

Some trucks race around the hill. The green truck drives up the hill like a ramp!

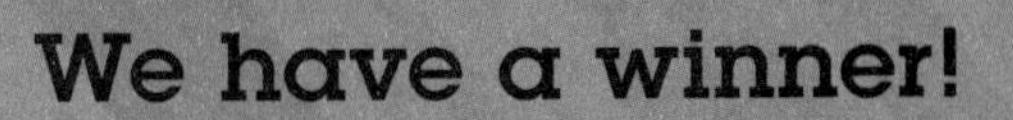

We have a winner!

THE SORRICK PTA
WISHES YOU A VERY
HAPPY BIRTHDAY!!!

SCHOLASTIC READER
1
LEVEL
HOT WHEELS™
Off-Roading
68
vandRvate
HOT WHEELS
Excellent
SCHOLASTIC